Holiday Mania at the House of Fun

Also by Jon Blake,
published by Hodder Children's Books:

The Deadly Secret of Dorothy W.
The Mad Mission of Jasmin J.

And more adventures
with Stinky and friends:

Stinky Finger's House of Fun
Crazy Party at the House of Fun
Mystery Guest at the House of Fun

Holiday Mania at the House of Fun

Jon Blake

illustrated by
David Roberts

A division of Hachette Children's Books

First published in Great Britain in 2007
by Hodder Children's Books

1

A Catalogue record for this book is available from the British Library

ISBN-10: 0 340 93129 9
ISBN-13: 9780340931295

Printed and bound in Great Britain by
Bookmarque Ltd, Croydon, Surrey

The paper and board used in this paperback by Hodder Children's Books are natural recyclable products made from wood grown in sustainable forests. The manufacturing processes conform to the environmental regulations of the country of origin.

Hodder Children's Books
A division of Hachette Children's Books
338 Euston Road, London NW1 3BH

Before We Begin

First let me introduce myself. I am Blue Soup. If you already know all about me, I strongly suggest you skip this bit and get on with the story. If you don't, what took you so long to find me?

As I was saying, I am Blue Soup. I tell stories. I also light up cities, provide hot dinners, and make that little thing in the top of the toilet go FZZZZZZZ. In fact, I make *everything* work, so no one has to waste their time being a cleaner, or an estate agent, or an MP.

What am I, you ask? Well, I'm not a person, that's obvious. Or a team of people. Or a computer virus. But please don't waste your time trying to imagine me, because you can't, just like you can't imagine the end of time, or what's beyond the very last star. If you do try to imagine me, first you will get a headache, then your head will explode.

As you've probably guessed, I come from Outer Space. Beyond the very last star, in fact. I was brought here by the Spoonheads. The Spoonheads are what you call aliens, except to them, you are aliens, and pretty weird ones at that.

Anyway, enough of me. This is the fourth story of Stinky Finger, who was first described in *Stinky Finger's House of Fun*. There are no grown-ups in Stinky's world. They've all been sucked up into the Space Zoo by the Spoonheads. That's why Stinky and his friends are in charge of the House of Fun, where something mad or dangerous is always around the corner …

… as you are about to discover.

Chapter One

Wacky House was a picture of disaster. Widget had just eaten the food that was meant for Whiffy's cat, and Neville Nerd had laughed so hard he'd fallen out of the window.

"Mouthwash!" cried Widget, racing around in manic circles.

"Here you go, dude!" cried Whiffy, handing him the cat. There was a huge gust of laughter. Everyone knew that "Mouthwash" was also the name of Whiffy's cat.

Note from Blue Soup:

You, on the other hand, have never heard of Mouthwash, or Whiffy, or Widget, or Neville Nerd, or Wacky House. Do not panic. All will be revealed.

Widget was dumbstruck. He didn't know what to do with the cat, so he put him in the bread bin. There was another gust of laughter. Widget looked round and seemed puzzled. "What happened to Neville?" he asked.

"Oh, nothing much," replied Whiffy. "He just fell out of the window."

There was a mild titter.

"Of all the dumb things that guy has done," added Whiffy, "*that* was the dumbest."

The titter grew to an excited laugh. Neville Nerd had come back in and was standing right behind Whiffy, covered in garbage.

"Isn't that guy the dumbest dumbhead you've met in your life?" continued Whiffy.

"Er ... Whiffy ..." warned Widget, trying unsuccessfully to signal to Whiffy that Neville was in the room.

"He thinks he's so smart," continued Whiffy. "Well, I bet he smarts now! Eh, Widget?" Whiffy turned. "Eh, Neville?" he added. "Neville!" he yelled.

The laughter grew to a roar.

"I so do not like this house!" said Neville,

and the laughter turned to applause, because everyone recognised the world-famous Wacky House catchphrase.

"CUT!" cried a firm girly voice. "OK, everybody, it's a wrap!"

At this, all the camera-people packed up their cameras, all the sound-people packed up their sound, and the audience trooped off home, still buzzing with excitement at seeing the last-ever episode of Wacky House.

Stinky Finger took off his Whiffy wig and breathed a sigh of relief. "Is it really over, Icky?" he asked.

Icky Bats, Stinky's great mate, unbuttoned his Widget waistcoat. "It really is," he replied.

"How many episodes did we do?" asked Stinky.

Icky counted on his fingers. "One ... two ... three hundred and forty-seven," he replied.

"I thought I was tired," said Stinky.

"I'm sorry it's over," said Bryan Brain. The third housemate of the House of Fun removed his thick-rimmed bottle-lensed glasses to show two very-slightly-moist eyes. Bryan had enjoyed playing Neville Nerd, especially after he got a fan letter, which he'd proudly displayed next to the three thousand, two hundred and fifty letters to Icky and Stinky.

"At least we won't have to talk American any more," said Icky.

"We sure won't," replied Stinky.

"Stinky," said Icky, "you're still doing it."

"Gee, I'm sorry," replied Stinky.

It was obviously going to take time to get everything back to normal, not that anything was that normal in the House of Fun.

"Bye folks!" said Ranking Susan, the director of Wacky House. "Thanks for giving us an Aim in Life!"

"Any time," said Icky, as director and crew exited the House of Fun for the three hundred and forty-seventh and last time.

There was a short silence, while Bryan pondered, Icky wandered, and Stinky gazed vacantly at the wild blue yonder. He had been bothered by an itch in his ear for some while now, and no matter how often he scratched it, it refused to go away.

"So," said Bryan. "What are we going to do now?"

"Well, personally," replied Icky. I need a ... a ..."

"What is it, Icky?" asked Stinky.

The idea was so exciting, Icky could hardly bring himself to spit it out. "A ... a ... a ... holiday!" he spluttered.

"Yes!" cried Stinky. "A holiday!" Dimly he remembered far-off days, before the Spoonheads came, days of buckets and spikes and jelly frisbees on a stick.

"But if we want a holiday," said Bryan, "we can go to the Super Safari Viewing Lounge."

The Super Safari Viewing Lounge was one of the many bizarre and magical rooms of the House of Fun. At the press of a button in this lounge, the housemates could conjure up China, the Arctic or Tunbridge Wells.

"But there's no *people* in the Super Safari Viewing Lounge," complained Stinky.

"Suits me," replied Bryan.

"Besides," said Icky, "you can only go so far, then you run into that invisible force field."

"I like the force field," mused Stinky. "It tingles."

"But it's not like going to the beach," said Icky, "and making sandcastles, and popping seaweed, and doing flick-flacks on the sewage pipe."

Stinky was all for that. Bryan still pretended to be doubtful, but secretly the idea of popping seaweed had got him quite excited. He had never been allowed to do that kind of thing when his parents were around.

"Let's pack!" cried Icky. As usual, he had to get going straight away, or if possible sooner. Within a minute he was at the front door, clutching a small plastic bag, waiting impatiently for the others. After what seemed an age Bryan appeared, bearing a beige canvas haversack, followed by Stinky, towing the most ginormous suitcase in the universe.

"I couldn't decide what to take," he explained. "So I brought everything."

Icky sighed. "This is all you need, Stinky," he said, opening his small plastic bag and revealing its contents. "A spare pair of pants ... a toothbrush ... trunks ... and a tube of Uberglue for emergencies."

"Spare pair of pants?" said Stinky. "You've got *two* pairs of pants?"

"That's right, Stinky," replied Icky, as patiently as possible.

Stinky counted on his fingers. "So that's four altogether," he said.

"No, Stinky," replied Icky. "It doesn't quite work like that. You don't have one pant, do you?"

"I do," said Stinky.

Icky thought it best not to pursue the matter. "Have you got your trunks, Bryan?" he asked instead.

As usual, Bryan hadn't been listening to a word. "Why do I need a trunk?" he said. "I've got a haversack."

"Not that kind of trunk, Bryan!" scoffed Icky.

At this, Stinky cheered up no end. It was someone else's turn to be stupid. "Not that kind of trunk, Bryan!" he echoed.

Icky and Stinky both doubled up laughing.

"I meant …" began Icky.

"… the kind you pick up buns with!" added Stinky.

Icky stopped laughing. "No, Stinky," he said. "Actually, I meant the kind of trunks you wear for swimming."

Stinky's face fell. "Couldn't you use those for picking up buns?" he asked hopefully.

"I suppose you could if you really tried," replied Icky.

"I thought so," muttered Stinky.

"Now let's see what's in this suitcase, shall we?" said Icky.

Stinky sheepishly unlocked the suitcase. Icky began unpacking the contents.

"A cuckoo clock," he began. "Will that be useful on holiday?"

"It could be," protested Stinky.

"But it doesn't even work!" said Icky.

"It just needs winding up," replied Stinky.

"You need winding up," murmured Bryan.

Icky pulled out the next item. "A bag of plant fertiliser," he announced.

Stinky couldn't really defend that one. "We'll leave that one out," he conceded.

"A meat thermometer," continued Icky. "A roll of embossed vinyl wallpaper. A ten-pack of small bone treats for dogs."

"I use them for scratching my ear," mumbled Stinky unconvincingly. "I've got this itch, see?"

"A pair of matching his-and-hers charm bracelets," continued Icky. "A lemon squeezer. A tutu and matching tights. An ornamental glass paperweight. Two bathroom taps."

"Did I pack two?" asked Stinky. "I only meant to put one in."

"Stinky," declared Icky. "This is not a holiday suitcase. It is a jumble sale suitcase."

"Shall we do that instead?" suggested Stinky.

"No!" cried Bryan, who had taken over as the impatient one. "Let's leave the case and go!"

"All right," said Stinky, slightly downcast. "I'll just take what you're taking, Icky, except without the Uberglue, toothbrush, trunks and spare pants, because I haven't got any of them."

"OK, Stinky," said Icky "Here's your plastic bag. Now let's **GO-O-O-O-O-O-O-O**!"

With that, Icky flung open the front door. Holiday time at last!

Chapter Two

"Has anyone got the front door key?" asked Stinky.

"I've never used the front door key," replied Icky.

"I never knew there *was* a front door key," said Bryan.

"We can't go on holiday without locking the front door," said Stinky. He reflected for a moment, then a small dim light came into his eyes. "I think I know where I left it," he announced.

Icky and Bryan were not convinced. It wasn't like Stinky to think, or know, and certainly not to think he knew.

"Where's that, Stinky?" asked Icky.

"The little curly cabinet," replied Stinky.

Icky frowned. "The little curly cabinet in the Living Living Room?" he asked.

"That's the one," said Stinky.

"Stinky," said Icky. "You should never leave anything in the Living Living Room!"

This was certainly true. Who would trust a room where the chairs grabbed your legs and the telly turned you into a potato?

"I thought it would be safe in there," said Stinky, "because no one would dare to get it."

"Yeah," said Icky. "Including us."

"I never thought of that," mumbled Stinky.

"Never mind," said Icky. "We'll just have to be very, very careful."

The three housemates of the House of Fun tiptoed warily into the perilous lounge. As always, there were a lot of sinister beeps and buzzes, topped off by the excited squeaks of Dronezone, once a world-famous boy band, now a not-so-famous pile of potatoes.

"Sorry, boys," whispered Stinky. "We're busy."

The curly cabinet sat at the far end of the room, alone. It was a small and beautiful object, well aware of its own good looks. Four curvy legs led up to a bow-fronted door with mother-of-pearl inlay, and above that a little bow-fronted drawer.

According to Stinky, the key was in that drawer.

"We could just rush it," suggested Icky.

"For that," replied Bryan, "we would need the Element of Surprise. And seeing as we are standing right here in the open, that element is sadly lacking."

"I think we should try stroking it," suggested Stinky.

"I beg your pardon?" replied Bryan.

"If we just gently dust it on top," explained Stinky, "it might put it in a good mood."

"It's worth a try," said Icky.

The three mates tiptoed softly up to the cabinet.

"I've got a hanky in my pocket," whispered Stinky. "Shall we use that?"

"Is it soft enough to dust with?" asked Icky doubtfully.

"I don't know," replied Stinky. "I'd have to get it open first."

"I think we'll use my hanky, thank you," said Bryan hastily. He reached into his pocket and produced a neatly folded white linen handkerchief with the letters BB embroidered in the corner. For a moment he seemed about to start dusting, then

came to his senses and handed the hanky to Stinky.

Stinky brought the hanky nervously down on to the top of the cabinet and began describing small gentle circles on the varnished wood.

A distinct purring noise rose up.

"It likes it!" whispered Icky.

Stinky dusted on. The purring grew louder.

"We've got it where we want it!" said Icky. He reached for the little drawer, but as he did so, the cabinet gave out a low, sinister growl.

"Maybe not," said Stinky.

"What if we polish its legs?" suggested Icky.

"Rather you than me," replied Bryan.

Icky pulled down the sleeve of his jumper and began shining away at one of the curly legs beneath the cabinet. The growling stopped. A gentle twittering began. Slowly, magically, the drawer began to open of its own accord.

"Quick, Bryan!" hissed Icky. "Get the key!"

"Why me?" rasped Bryan.

"We're dusting!" hissed Icky.

As if reaching into a fire, Bryan's trembly hand hovered upwards, then dipped like a wren's beak into the drawer. The twittering stopped. The low growl returned.

"There's nothing in here!" cried Bryan.

The growl got a little louder.

"Are you sure, Bryan?" asked Stinky.

"Positive!" hissed Bryan.

The growl got louder still.

"Hmm," said Bryan. "I think I'd better—"

SLAM!

The drawer snapped back like a mousetrap. Amazingly, Bryan's hand moved even faster. "Aha!"

he yelled. "I was ready for you, see!" He turned in triumph to Icky. "Did you see that, Icky?" he said.

"Aa ... aa ... aa ..." replied Icky, an agonised look on his face.

To Bryan's amazement, while his own hand was safe, Icky's was stuck firmly in the drawer.

"I ... I ... just wanted to ch-check," stammered Icky.

Stinky inspected Icky's trapped hand with a look of concern. "Does it hurt, Icky?" he asked thoughtfully.

"Y-yes," trembled Icky. "It ________ does."

Note from Blue Soup:

I do not have Icky's exact words within my language database, but perhaps you can imagine them for yourselves.

"Do you want us to get you out of there, Ick?" asked Stinky.

"T-that would be n-nice," grunted Icky.

"Let's try dusting again," said Stinky.

Stinky went back to work on the top of the cabinet and Bryan tickled the legs. After a while the cabinet began purring again, but Icky's hand stayed stuck fast. This went on for several minutes, and as it had been a tiring day, Bryan couldn't stifle a yawn. At this, Stinky also yawned, and despite his agony, Icky followed that with a yawn of his own. Of course, this often happens with people, but it was quite a surprise when a strange creak came from the cabinet and the drawer miraculously opened. Icky was free.

"Brilliant idea, Bryan!" said Stinky.

"It was nothing," replied Bryan, which was true enough.

Icky inspected his hand, which now had a sinister red valley running across the fingers. "I wouldn't have minded," he said, "if we'd got the key."

"Hmm," said Stinky thoughtfully. "Come to think of it, I never put it there in the first place."

"*What?*" growled Icky.

"I've just remembered," said Stinky. "I was *going* to put it here, then I heard a noise, so I went upstairs to the gym."

"The gym?" repeated Icky. "You mean the Random Madness Gym?"

"That's the one," replied Stinky.

"Stinky," said Icky, "tell me you didn't leave the key in the Random Madness Gym."

"I didn't leave the key in the Random Madness Gym," pronounced Stinky. "Except I did," he added.

This was even worse news. The Random Madness Gym was the most unpredictable room in the House of Fun. Things could be perfectly normal in there all afternoon, then the most extreme and scary changes could come over the housemates in an instant. Icky still had a fear of spoons from the time he thought his head was a boiled egg, and he wasn't keen to repeat the experience.

"I can't do gym," he said. "My hand hurts."

"Nor me," said Bryan. "I've got a verruca."

"What's a verruca?" asked Stinky.

"It's a big white wart on your foot with an ugly black spot in the middle," replied Bryan.

"My feet are covered in those," said Stinky. "Doesn't stop me doing gym."

Bryan pretended not to hear.

"Do you want to see?" asked Stinky. He began peeling back one of his matted old socks.

"All right!" cried Bryan. "I'll go to the flipping gym!"

Chapter Three

At first sight, the Random Madness Gym was just like a typical school gym. It smelled of sweaty feet and rubber mats, and there was always one tatty old plimsoll left abandoned on a bench. In one corner was a beast of a gym horse, with a broken trampette leaning against it. Wooden climbing frames ran up the side walls, alongside a set of climbing ropes which could be winched out across the room. High above, the ceiling was dotted with hanging rings, and at the far end was a basketball hoop with a ropey old net dangling off it.

"So," said Bryan. "Where did you put the key, Stinky?"

"In the plimsoll," replied Stinky with great certainty.

Bryan looked around. Unusually, the skaggy pump was nowhere to be seen. "And where is the plimsoll?" he asked.

"Somewhere safe," replied Stinky.

"And where, pray, is that?" asked Bryan.

"There," said Stinky. He pointed up to the far end of the gym. High up.

"The basketball net?" asked Bryan worriedly.

"Good shot, eh?" said Stinky.

Bryan approached the hoop and looked up. Sure enough, there was the skaggy pump, tangled up in the ropey net. "Were you having an episode of Random Madness?" he enquired.

"Maybe," replied Stinky.

"Let's hope so," said Bryan.

"It's going to be hard to get down," said Stinky.

"Indeed," replied Bryan.

The two mates surveyed the scene. Yes, they could climb up the climbing frame on the side wall. But that still left at least ten metres to the hoop. The only way to get across that was by the hanging rings.

"Shall we toss for it?" asked Stinky.

"Don't bother," replied Bryan. The housemates

had tossed for things at least twenty times, and drawn straws at least thirty, and Bryan was still searching for his first win. Still, if it was a hero they needed, Superyawn was clearly the man.

"Good luck, Bry," said Stinky, hoisting Bryan up on to the frame.

Bryan was not a natural climber. He climbed the bars one at a time, like a little hobbling old man. He held fast at all times with both hands, so had no way of stopping his specs sliding down his nose, except tipping back his head like a braying moose. When he finally reached the top, he viewed the first hanging ring with despair.

"Stinky," he said, "I'm scared."

"Don't worry, Bry!" yelled Stinky. "I'm right underneath you."

Bryan chanced a quick look down, just in time to see Stinky pushing the trampette into position beneath him. "Ah well," thought Bryan. "At least I won't die straight away. At least I'll bounce first."

"You can do it, Bry!" yelled Stinky.

Bryan stretched out as far as he could. His trembling fingers snaked weakly around the ring.

Unfortunately, however, his trembling feet lost their grip the next second. Bryan seized the ring like a last straw and wound up dangling by one arm six metres above the ground.

"Haa! Aaah! Aaah! Aaaah!" he squealed.

"Keep swinging, Bryan!" called Stinky. "Keep swinging, or you'll never reach the next one!"

Bryan did indeed keep swinging, forward, back, left, right, while his cries grew shriller and shriller.

"Aa! Aaa! Oooo! Oooo! Hu-hu-hu-hu-hu!"

At this point something quite miraculous happened. Bryan's spare hand swung up and caught hold of the next ring. For a moment he stayed stretched between the rings, like the victim of some strange torture, before letting go of the first one and dangling safely from the second.

"Well done, Bryan!" yelled Stinky. "That was frabjous!"

Bryan was not finished yet. He swung athletically from the second ring to the third and then, to Stinky's amazement, let go with both hands and swung gracefully through the air to the next. "Hu-huu! Huu, huu, huu, huu!" he called. It was a sound which reminded Stinky vaguely of a nature film he'd watched many years before – a film about some weird animals which looked a bit like people and had a dangerously long name.

"Huu! Huu! Huu!" cried Bryan, as he swung effortlessly now from ring to ring, before finally clutching hold of the basketball hoop, fishing inside, and emerging triumphantly with the skaggy plimsoll, which he flung to the floor with gay abandon.

Stinky seized the plimsoll. Yes! The key was still inside!

"You did it, Bry!" he cried.

Bryan's only answer was to beat his chest and let out a series of high-pitched cackles. He began to make his way back across the rings, swinging as easy and smooth as a pendulum, before leaping from the last one to the climbing frame, scrabbling down that with amazing speed, and setting off across the floor towards Stinky.

Oddly, however, Bryan chose to do this not on two feet, but on four, with the knuckles of his hands brushing the floor as he lolloped across.

"Hu hu hu hu hu!" he cried.

"Are you all right, Bryan?" asked Stinky.

Bryan's only reply was to leap at his housemate with both hands and feet, to end up clinging beneath him like a great dangling rucksack. No matter how hard Stinky struggled, Bryan would not let go, till Stinky had to drop to his own hands and knees under the weight.

At this point there was a cry from Icky: "Did you get the key, Stinky?"

"Y-yes!" replied Stinky. "B-but I've got a bit of a problem with B-Bryan!"

"Is it serious?" called Icky.

"Quite serious," replied Stinky. "What was the name of that funny animal, the one that looked like a hairy person?"

"A chimpanzee?" asked Icky.

"That's the one," said Stinky. With an enormous effort he managed to lollop across the gym, Bryan clinging fast, before hauling open the door and presenting Icky with the bizarre spectacle. "Bryan thinks he's a chimpanzee," he explained.

Icky considered the situation. He wasn't that surprised. Worse things had happened in the Random Madness Gym. "Have you tried getting him off?" he asked.

"You can try if you like," said Stinky.

"Come on, Bryan," said Icky. Icky reached towards Bryan, but as he did so, Bryan drew back his gums, bared his teeth, and unleashed a stream of cackles quite scary in their intensity.

"I think we'd better leave him there for now," suggested Stinky.

"Is he heavy?" asked Icky.

"Yes," said Stinky, "but also strangely comforting."

Icky led the way downstairs, with Stinky lumbering behind, Bryan swinging from side to side beneath him like an overstuffed bag of shopping. They finally reached the front door and Stinky produced the magic key.

"Frabjous," said Icky. "Where's the keyhole?"

The two mates scanned the door from left to right and top to bottom but could find no sign of a key-shaped hole.

"If there's a key," pronounced Stinky, "there *must* be a keyhole."

Icky began to fear the worst.

"Stinky," he said. "This key you hid so carefully. Are you sure it was for the door?"

"What else could it have been for?" asked Stinky.

For some reason, Icky's eyes fell on the cuckoo clock. "Stinky," he said. "Tell me the key isn't actually for that clock."

"The key isn't actually for that clock," repeated Stinky.

"It is, isn't it?" asked Icky.

"Maybe," replied Stinky.

Icky tried the key in the cuckoo-clock's winding-hole, and sure enough, it fitted perfectly.

"Sorry," said Stinky.

Icky beat his head softly against the wall for a while, then considered practical matters.

"How did we get into this house in the first place?" he asked.

Stinky thought back. For some reason Stinky was better at thinking back than thinking forwards or sideways, not that that was saying much. "I just came up the steps," he said, "looked through the peephole, then opened the door."

"Hmm," said Icky. "Maybe looking through the peephole unlocked the door."

"Dunno," said Stinky. "I've never looked through it since."

"Ah," said Icky. "Maybe if you did, it would lock it again."

"Worth a try," said Stinky.

Icky opened the door and Stinky lumbered outside, still with Bryan clinging tight beneath him. It wasn't easy for Stinky to stand up, but with a great effort he finally made it, just high enough to put his eye to the peephole.

CLUNK!

"It worked!" cried Icky, from inside. "Now try again, Stinky!"

UNCLUNK!

"Ducks deluxe!" cried Icky. "We've cracked it!"

Stinky lumbered back inside with Bryan, while Icky decided to check if it worked for him as well. Sure enough, the door locked as he pressed his eye to the peephole, then unlocked as he did it again. A worrying thought came to Icky. What if the door unlocked for *anyone* who put their eye to the peephole?

It didn't take Icky long to solve this problem. It was a solution so brilliant that he marched back inside with his fist in the air then did a complete victory lap of the house.

Returning to the front door, Icky was surprised to find Stinky standing upright and completely alone.

"Great news," said Stinky. "Bryan's gone back to normal."

"Never mind that!" said Icky. "Listen to what I did! I was worried, see, in case other people could unlock the door, so I stuck some Uberglue round the peephole! Of course, we'll have to be very careful when we use it, not to press our eyes right up to it! Where is Bryan, by the way?"

"Testing the peephole," replied Stinky.

There was a howl of anguish from the other side of the door.

"Uh-oh," said Icky.

Chapter Four

Fans of the House of Fun will know that this was not the first time Bryan had been stuck to a door. However, it was the first time he'd been stuck to a door by his eye, and he wasn't enjoying the experience one bit.

"Do you want us to try to pull you off?" asked Stinky.

"No!" cried Bryan.

"Is it the actual eye that's stuck," asked Icky, "or just the lid?"

"I-I can't tell," stammered Bryan.

Icky sighed. It was so typical of Bryan to spoil it when they were about to have fun. He took Stinky quietly to one side. "We could cover him with a tarpaulin," he suggested.

"What good will that do?" asked Stinky.

"It'll keep the rain off him while we're on holiday," replied Icky.

"Icky," said Stinky. "We can't go on holiday while Bryan's stuck to the door."

Deep down, Icky knew Stinky was right, but further up, his patience was wearing thin. "If we don't go soon," he complained, "it'll be winter!"

"Could we maybe take Bryan *and* the door?" suggested Stinky.

Deep down, Icky knew this was a really stupid idea, but further up, he was willing to do anything to get away. "OK," he replied. "Let's do it."

The two housemates fetched the house tools, selected a suitable screwdriver, and got to work on the door hinges.

"What's going on?" bleated Bryan.

"Just stay there and leave it all to us," replied Icky.

"I wasn't thinking of going anywhere," said Bryan.

Icky worked hammer and tongs at the door hinges, despite only having a screwdriver. Soon only one screw was holding the door to the door frame.

"OK, Stinky," he said. "Now stand behind the door and take the weight as it comes off."

Stinky did as instructed. Unfortunately, however, Icky had forgotten that the weight of the door was closely followed by the weight of Bryan. As the whole lot crashed to the ground, all that could be seen of Stinky was his left foot.

"Uh-oh," said Icky.

"What happened?" said Bryan.

"Nnnnggghhhurrrrrarrgh," said Stinky.

With all his strength, Icky prised the door just high enough for Stinky to crawl out. "Are you all right, Stinky?" he asked.

"I heard something snap," replied Stinky.

"Uh-oh," said Icky. "What do you think it was?"

"I'm not sure," said Stinky. "I think it may have been my hanky."

"*What's going on?*" squealed Bryan.

"It's all right, Bryan," said Icky. "We're taking you on holiday."

"Actually," said Stinky, "I've gone off that idea. Bryan's heavier than he looks."

Icky searched for a new idea, and as usual, took the first one which arrived. "OK," he suggested. "How about this. We put Bryan in the Time Travel Van, then go back to just before I put the Uberglue on the peephole."

A red warning light began to flash urgently in Stinky's brain. He often got this light when Icky had an idea, especially when it involved time travel.

"Hmm," he said. "Is that wise?"

"Got any better ideas?" asked Icky.

"Come on then," said Stinky.

The two mates took hold of the door, one at each end, and with considerable effort lifted it, and Bryan, into the air.

"*What's going on?*" squealed Bryan, who was in such a state of panic, he hadn't taken in a word the others had said.

"Relax, Bryan," said Icky as they barged into the Time Travel Garage. "We'll have you fixed in a jiffy."

Bryan was not reassured. A bull terrier had threatened to fix him once, when there wasn't anything wrong with him at all, and it was not a good memory.

"One ... two ... three ... HEAVE!" cried Icky, as Bryan, and the door, were loaded into the back of the Time Travel Van.

"I hope we're not in the Time Travel Van!" blabbered Bryan.

"Would we be that stupid?" said Icky. "Stick the seat belt on him, Stinky."

Luckily the Time Travel Van was designed like a taxi, with a soundproof pane of glass between the front cab and the back. Once Icky and Stinky were in the cab they couldn't hear a thing, though they could still see Bryan's fists hammering frantically on his door.

"I've just thought of something," said Stinky.

"What?" said Icky, impatiently.

"We've left the front door wide open," replied Stinky.

"How can it be wide open?" said Icky. "It's in the back of the van."

"That's true," said Stinky. "But there's still a big hole where it used to be."

"Relax," said Icky. "We'll be back before we left."

"Ah," said Stinky. He wasn't entirely convinced, but his head was starting to spin, so he studied the time-slider instead. "Where did you say we were going?" he asked.

"To ten minutes ago," said Icky.

"The time-slider hasn't got Ten Minutes Ago on it," replied Stinky.

"What's the closest thing to it?" asked Icky.

"1936," replied Stinky.

"We'll switch off the Auto and go over to Manual," declared Icky.

"OK," replied Stinky. Of course, he really had no idea what this meant, but then, neither did Icky.

He'd just noticed a switch on the dashboard with **AUTO** and **MANUAL** written on it, which he now flicked from one to the other.

"Now we just press this button," said Icky confidently, noticing a big green button under the word **MANUAL**.

"How long for?" asked Stinky.

"A very, very short time," replied Icky. "Then we'll go a very, very short way."

"Sounds good to me," said Stinky.

"OK," said Icky. "Let's draw straws to see who presses it."

Stinky suddenly didn't feel so confident. "Why?" he asked. But Icky already had the straws in his hand.

Stinky duly drew the short one.

"Now remember," said Icky. "A very, very short push."

"OK," said Stinky, "but don't put me off by saying 'Are We There Yet?' like you always do when we time travel."

"Scout's honour," replied Icky.

Stinky drew a deep breath, lifted a shaky pointy finger, and jabbed. Unfortunately, however, he had forgotten one crucial thing: the bogey which had been on the end of his pointy finger since breakfast. Despite Icky's frantic yells, Stinky's finger stayed stuck firmly to the button. By the time he finally pulled it free, they had sailed through at least a century.

"Sorry," he said. "Shall I try to get us back to Ten Minutes Ago?"

This, of course, would have been the sensible thing to do, but naturally enough, Icky had other plans. "Let's just see where we are," he said. "We might be near a Glue Removal Clinic or something."

Unfortunately, however, they were in the middle of a wood.

"Can you hear singing?" asked Icky.

Stinky strained his ears, which was a bit like straining potatoes, owing to the large amounts of gunk inside them. "Yes," he said. "It sounds like lots of people, or one person with lots of voices."

"If there's lots of people," said Icky, "one of

them is bound to have something for removing eyes from doors."

"That's true," said Stinky.

"Let's get Bryan out and track them down," said Icky.

Icky and Stinky hauled Bryan from the Time Travel Van, still stuck firmly to the door, but quiet now, knackered from all the screaming and hammering. The three mates began to make their way through the wood, guided only by the voices, which seemed to grow younger as they grew louder. It was hard work, especially for Stinky, as his ear had become particularly itchy, and it was impossible for him to scratch it.

Eventually the wood thinned out and gave way to a hill thick with thistles. Icky and Stinky ploughed on, yowwing and owwing and arrghing towards the distant crest. Icky loved crests, because you never knew what was over them. Stinky feared them for exactly the same reason.

But neither expected the view that greeted them over this particular crest.

"What *are* they?" asked Stinky.

"Aliens," replied Icky, with great certainty.

"Not ... Spoonheads?" asked Stinky.

"Hatheads," replied Icky.

The strange beings, of which there were at least fifty, began a new song, which they sang with huge enthusiasm:

"We're riding along on the crest of a wave
And the sun is in the sky!
All of our eyes on the distant horizon,
Look out for passers-by!"

Icky and Stinky had never seen anyone dressed like these creatures. They wore green caps, yellow neckerchiefs and baggy shorts down to their knees. Their shirts were covered in strange badges and their shoes were sensible and brown. The whole troop were gathered close to a river, watched over by larger aliens with bigger hats, who stood beside a variety of makeshift rafts made of planks and barrels and rope.

"Actually," said Stinky, "they look a bit like people."

"Let's find out," said Icky.

The two housemates headed down into the river valley, bearing Bryan like a sick missionary.

"Hail!" cried Icky. "We come in peace!"

The singing stopped. The troop turned as one towards the housemates. One of the larger ones called out: "Are you for the race?"

"What did he say?" asked Stinky.

"Just keep smiling," said Icky.

The larger Hathead strode forward to greet the housemates. He seemed very fit and wiry, but closer up, looked quite old and had a rather unsettling little moustache. "So," he said, "which pack are you from?"

"The House of Fun pack," replied Icky.

"House of Fun pack?" repeated the old Hathead. "Haven't heard of them. Do you have a pack song?"

"Yes," replied Icky.

"Have we?" said Stinky.

"Let's hear it," barked old Hathead.

Icky didn't need a second invitation. After lowering Bryan to the ground a little too quickly, he began wheeling his arm in faster and faster circles as if building up energy for a lengthy jump. Suddenly, a banshee wail escaped his lips:

"Show me a big fat armadillo!

I've got a fish beneath my pillow!

Dreaming dreams of armadillos!

And sweaty Pete the centipede!"

The singing stopped and Icky's whirling arm came slowly to a standstill. The entire troop of Hatheads stood in stunned silence.

"It just came to me," Icky whispered to Stinky.

"So," said old Hathead, viewing the door at the housemates' feet. "This is your raft, is it?"

"Yes," replied Icky.

"What's that fellow doing?" asked the old Hathead, indicating Bryan.

"Keeping an eye on it," replied Icky.

Old Hathead shook his head grimly. "In my opinion," he said, "it would be very unwise to put this craft in the river."

"All right then," said Icky. "We won't."

"Nonsense!" snapped Old Hathead. "I'll get some of my boys to help you make it seaworthy. A Wolf Cub never shirks a challenge."

With that, old Hathead marched back to his pack

and started giving orders left right and centre.

"What's going on?" squeaked Bryan.

Icky and Stinky gave no answer, mainly because they didn't have an answer to give.

Chapter Five

A tall lad with eagle eyes and a fat nose stood before Icky and Stinky. "Hello," he said. "I'm George, and I'm the Supersixer here, so you'd better bally well do what I say."

Icky decided it was time to be honest. "Actually," he said, "we don't want to be in a raft race. Our friend is stuck to the door by his eye and we wondered if you could get him off."

"Hmm," said George. "That's a tough one. Akela has told me to help you with the raft, so I *must* do that, but if I helped your friend, that would be breaking my Wolf Cub Promise."

"Wolf Cub Promise?" repeated Stinky. "What's that?"

George stood to attention. "I promise to do my

best," he declared, "to do my duty to God and the King, and to do a good turn to somebody every day."

Icky and Stinky were confused. They'd never heard of God-and-the-King, and if Bryan got a good turn he'd have the door on top of him.

"Which bit would you be breaking?" asked Icky.

"Well," said George. "If I helped you with the raft *and* helped you unstick your friend, I'd be doing *two* good turns."

Icky and Stinky looked at each other. "*Can* you get Bryan off the door?" asked Icky.

"Oh yes," replied George. His voice dropped to a whisper: "I've got a scout knife."

"Wow," said Stinky, who had no idea what this was.

George took a glance behind him, then dug into his pocket and produced an interesting-looking implement. It was shaped like a small harmonica and had a whole range of useful tools folded away inside it, which George levered out one by one. "Screwdriver … can opener … corkscrew … scissors … nailfile … toothpick … tweezers … thing for getting stones out of horses' hooves … thing for getting eyes unstuck from doors."

"That's the one!" cried Icky.

George thought for a moment. "I'll tell you what," he said. "As Supersixer, it is my job to inspire you to Do Your Best. If, therefore, you win the raft race, I shall unstick your friend from the door."

"OK," said Icky.

"Is it?" said Stinky.

"Let's get to work on this raft," said George.

The housemates had to hand it to George. He knew how to build a raft. He selected some barrels and lashed them to the door with some stout rope, taking care not to step on Bryan more than twice. Now and then Icky or Stinky tried to lend a hand,

but usually ended up with the hand lashed in with the barrels, such was the speed at which George worked.

"Now," he said, pulling the final rope tight. "Should I use a sheepshank, a clove hitch, or a cat's paw?"

"I'd just use the rope," suggested Icky.

George stopped work for a second. "Don't you know any knots?" he said.

"I know not to sit on a fire," said Stinky.

George frowned. "However did you get your tenderpads?" he asked.

"We trod on some thistles," replied Icky.

"What?" scoffed George. "You two don't know anything about anything!"

"We do!" protested Icky. "By the way, what year is it?"

George brought his face very close to Icky. He smelt of sweat and baked beans and the ink of a thousand boys' comics. "1937," he said.

"I knew that," said Icky.

George laughed, a great hawing guffaw, a bit like a donkey being sick. "You prize oaf!" he cried. "It's 1936!"

Icky had been wondering for a while whether he liked George, and now decided very firmly that he didn't. "You'd better keep your promise about unsticking Bryan," he growled.

"A Wolf Cub always keeps his promise," replied George. "Dyb dyb dyb dyb!"

"Eh?" said Icky.

"Dyb dyb dyb dyb!" repeated George.

"Do what?" said Stinky.

"You're supposed to go 'Dob dob dob dob'!" barked George.

"Why?" said Icky.

George's nostrils flared. "You're a disgrace to the Empire!" he cried.

"Whatever," said Icky.

George's mouth began to twitch in an alarming way. He turned on his heel and stormed back to the main troop. "Akela!" he declared. "Those two cubs are refusing to do the Grand Howl!"

"He's a funny bloke, that George," said Stinky.

"Yeah," growled Icky. "I'm going to *thrash* him."

"Thrash him?" repeated Stinky. "What with?"

"In the race, I mean!" rasped Icky.

Stinky had never seen Icky so worked up.

He pushed the raft to the riverbank as if his life depended on it and with a great shove heaved it single-handedly into the river, where, thankfully, it floated like a cork.

"What's going on?" bleated Bryan.

"Nothing to worry about," said Stinky, "but if you find yourself underwater, try not to breathe."

Icky and Stinky were handed a paddle each, which quickly became two paddles for Icky, who crouched at the ready with eyes of fire.

"You will start on my whistle," commanded old Hathead. "I shall then take up position by the willow tree before the weir, which will serve as the finish line. Now, what will you do?"

"Our best!" cried everybody.

"Which won't be good enough," growled Icky.

There was a shrill blast. Nine rafts set off furiously, but none as furiously as House of Fun One. Icky's paddles hammered the water like raindrops in a tropical storm, and in no time there was clear blue water between the housemates' raft and the opposition.

"Go easy, Ick," said Stinky. "Don't run out of puff."

Icky, however, was showing no sign of slowing down. If anything, he was getting stronger. Ducks scattered in squawking panic as his furious paddles bore down on them. House of Fun One careered round the first bend, two lengths clear of their nearest pursuer, pulling clearer by the second. Not that Icky had any idea what was behind. His eyes were fixed like lasers to the willow tree ahead.

"Is it much further?" groaned Bryan. "I'm getting sea-sick."

"Don't worry, Bryan," said Stinky. "We're home and dry."

"You may be dry," moaned Bryan, "but I am not."

Icky was deaf to everything. He mowed down a river in a shower of spray, soaking not only Bryan but the fleeing ducks, the damsel and dragonflies, and any afternoon strollers within spitting distance.

Suddenly, however, there was a cry from behind: "Good going, Dopey! Know what year it is yet?"

Icky stopped paddling. Two fiery eyes shot backwards, to see George the supersixer some way back, on the opposite side of the river, thumbing his nose.

"Don't stop, you ass!" cried George. "You might ... tread on a thistle!"

This, of course, was an extremely stupid and unfunny thing to say, but that made no difference to Icky. With a few carving strokes of the paddle, he turned House of Fun One round, and headed full-tilt for George's raft.

"Icky – no!" cried Stinky, but it was a lost cause. Icky was now set on teaching George a different kind of lesson. The river turned to total chaos as House of Fun One ploughed straight across the bows of two other rafts, missing them by millimetres, before taking a glancing blow off a third which sent House of Fun One wobbling like a wonky wheel. Still Icky bore down on his rival, but just as he got within splashing distance, George took evasive action. With a sudden spurt, he got the other side of House of Fun One, leaving Icky floundering in the wrong direction and panting for breath.

"Icky!" cried Stinky. "Forget George! Turn the raft round and go for the line!"

Icky, however, was spent. His mad dash across the river had drained all the energy out of him and left him dabbling his paddle like a doddering doo-dah. With a last weak effort he turned the raft, then dropped his head and closed his eyes.

"Icky!" cried Stinky, who believed his mate would always come through, and know what to do, and save the day, even if he didn't know what year it was.

"What's going on?" squealed Bryan.

Icky opened one eye. The hands had stopped but the brain was still working. "The others have panicked," he said.

"Panicked?" squeaked Bryan. "Why?"

"That thing," panted Icky. "You know, that big thing, like a lizard. Eats people."

"A crocodile?" asked Bryan.

"That's the one," said Icky.

"There's a crocodile in the river?" squealed Bryan.

"Right behind us," said Icky.

"Why aren't we moving?" bawled Bryan.

"I'm knackered," said Icky.

"What?" shrieked Bryan. "Give me the paddles!"

It is amazing what people can achieve when faced with the immediate possibility of death.

Despite being face-down on the door, Bryan's out-stretched arms began paddling with superhuman strength and speed, so much so that he caught and passed the rearmost rafts within half a minute.

"Where's the bank?" cried Bryan. "Why haven't we reached the bank?"

"Keep going!" cried Icky. "It's straight ahead!"

Of course, all that was really ahead was the finish-line and three enemy rafts. George was now out in front, coasting (or so he thought) to victory and a firm handshake from Akela. But George had not bargained for the phenomenon that was Bryan Brain. With fear for his life still coursing through his veins, Bryan whacked the water like a fleeing coot. Past the third raft ... past the second ...

"Come on, Bryan!" yelled Stinky. "You can win it!"

"Eh?" spluttered Bryan. "Win what?"

"Win ... the crocodile!" blithered Stinky.

"'Beat', not 'win'!" gasped Bryan. Bryan always had time to correct bad English, even when fleeing for his life.

George, meanwhile, savoured his moment of triumph. With the line just a few metres away, he turned to give a regal wave, only to see Bryan halfway alongside and still going like blazes. Too late, George returned to his paddle. With just millimetres to go, Bryan edged past and took the chequered flag, which was actually a Wolf Cub neckerchief, but just as glorious.

"You did it, Bryan!" cried Icky. "You did it!"

Bryan did not reply. Nor did he stop. With his face pressed against the door, Bryan was blissfully unaware of the finishing line. He was also completely blind to the humungous weir just a few metres ahead.

"Bryan!" cried Stinky. "Stop!"

"Too late, Stinky!" cried Icky. "Jump!"

The two housemates plunged into the water, surfacing just in time to see House of Fun One, and Bryan Brain, plunging over the lip of the weir.

Frantically they swam to the bank, scrambled out, and raced like demons after their friend. It really was a big weir, as they soon saw, with water shooting down to a churning watery chaos.

"There it is!" cried Icky, catching sight of House of Fun One, upside-down, twenty metres ahead, stuck between two boulders at the river's edge.

The two housemates ran, slid and scrambled towards the stricken raft, which had lost two of its barrels and was in danger of breaking up completely. A length of rope was hanging from its side, thrashing about in the churning river like a water snake.

"Hang on to me!" yelled Icky. He waded into the torrent, one hand grasped by Stinky, seized the end of the flailing rope, and tugged it back to shore. Together they hauled the rope, and with it House of Fun One, slowly to safety. As the raft reached the riverbank, they gave it a mighty heave, yanking it head-over-heels on to the grass to free their trapped housemate.

Except, horror of horrors, Bryan was not there.

Chapter Six

Note from Blue Soup:

This chapter begins about half a minute after the last one ended. You haven't missed much, except a lot of screaming and bawling from Icky and Stinky.

"It's hopeless," groaned Stinky. "He'll be miles down the river by now."

"If he's still … alive," murmured Icky.

"That's it," said a third voice. "Give up on me."

Icky and Stinky wheeled round in amazement to see their lost mate standing right behind them, like a half-drowned dog, grazed and bruised and battered, one paw held over the eye which had been stuck to the door.

"Bryan!" cried Stinky. "Are you all right?"

"Frabjous," replied Bryan. "Tickety-boo. Ducks deluxe. Where's this bleeping crocodile then?"

"How did you get off?" asked Icky, conveniently ignoring Bryan's question.

"I think it was when I hit the third rock," sneered Bryan.

"Is your eye all right?" asked Stinky.

"What eye?" asked Bryan.

"The eye you're hiding behind your hand," said Stinky.

"Oh," said Bryan. "That eye."

"It is ... still there?" asked Stinky nervously.

"I really don't know," replied Bryan. "Perhaps you'd like to take a look."

With that Bryan slowly and dramatically lowered his hand to reveal ...

Note from Blue Soup:

Here we must bid farewell to all readers under the age of sixteen. It's probably past your bedtime anyway. Or perhaps you're the rebellious type who makes a point of doing everything you're told not to do. In which case good luck to you and let's hope you don't grow up too twisted and damaged from what you are about to read after the child safety gap I am now inserting.

... something very vital missing.

"Bryan ..." stuttered Icky. "Your eye ... your eye ... your ... eyelashes."

"Ah," said Bryan. "That's what's gone. I thought I felt something rip."

"It looks kind of ... sore," noted Icky.

"Sore," repeated Bryan. "Yes, yes, it is rather sore."

"Quite funny though," added Stinky helpfully.

"I'm glad it amuses you," replied Bryan. "Can I go home now?"

"As soon as we've got our door back," said Icky. He began to untie the lashings, but as he did so, another hand took hold of the rope.

"Here," said a manly young voice, "let me help with that."

The hand belonged to George.

Note from Blue Soup:

The following scene did not really happen. I was asked to put it in by the producers of Wacky House, who are thinking of making a major motion picture featuring the housemates. If I were you I would skip it completely and go on to the next chapter.

"I guess I owe you guys an apology," said George.

"We're all ears," replied Widget.

"I underestimated you," said George. "I thought you were a bunch of hicks from the sticks without a hope in hell of cutting it with the big boys. But you really showed some class back there. Serious class."

George's eyes locked firmly on to Widget's. A wry smile played around Widget's mouth. "I guess I owe you an apology too," he said. "I was kind of hasty back there."

"Truce?" asked George, holding out a hand.

"Truce," replied Widget, shaking it.

"I may be a rough kind of diamond," continued George, "but I'm a guy who keeps his word." He produced his scout's knife. "Now, where's this pal of yours?"

"Neville?" asked Whiffy. "Why, he's right here!"

Neville Nerd stepped forward and gave a double thumbs-up. The whole company roared with laughter.

"But ..." spluttered George. "How did he ..."

"It's a long story," said Neville.

George returned the scout's knife to his pocket

and, in its place, drew out three beautiful new cloth badges. "Akela said to give you these," he announced. "Three Wolf Cub Raft Racing badges. Where do you want me to stick them?"

"Don't even ask!" quipped Neville, and the whole gang dissolved into laughter again. As one, they set off down the riverbank path towards the setting sun. Widget threw an arm around George's shoulder. "So tell me, George," he began, "do you really know 2000 knots?"

"Now that's another story," trilled George, as the four friends dissolved into drawings in a happy, hopeful children's book, which slowly closed to show the words TO BE CONTINUED.

Note from Blue Soup:

Not.

Chapter Seven

Icky hammered home the last screw and the front door of the House of Fun was back in place.

"There you go," he said. "Good as new."

"Are you supposed to use a hammer on screws?" asked Stinky.

"Course you are," replied Icky. "Unless you want to do it the *slow* way, and that would be *torture*." He shuddered at the thought. "Right," he said. "I'll just check I put it on the right way round." With a workman's whistle he sauntered out of the door, inspected it from the outside, then returned with a satisfied smile. "I'll just go to the bog," he said, "then we'll be off."

Bryan was unhappy. He waited for Icky to disappear then confided in Stinky. "The trouble is," he whispered, "I'm scared to use the peephole now, and if you two die on holiday, I won't be able to get back in."

"Hmm," said Stinky, who was always impressed by Bryan's ability to think of everything. "I remember someone saying, if you fall off a bike, the best idea is to get straight back on."

"And?" said Bryan.

"I don't know," said Stinky. "I just remember someone saying it."

"Ah!" said Bryan. "I get you. I should go out there now, stick my eye against the peephole, and get it over with."

"Yes, that's it," replied Stinky. "I think."

After the day's adventures, Bryan was feeling unusually bold. He did exactly as he suggested, closing the front door just as Icky reappeared on the scene.

"Where's Bryan?" asked Icky.

"Sticking his eye against the peephole," replied Stinky.

"What?" said Icky. "I've just put Uberglue round it again!"

"You're joking," said Stinky.

"Afraid not," said Icky.

At this point the door reopened and Bryan walked back in. "I didn't get too close this time," he said. "Imagine if I'd got my eye stuck again, how boring and tedious that would have been."

"Yes," agreed Stinky, "and not particularly funny either."

"Shall we go on holiday now?" suggested Icky.

"Yeah!" said Stinky, starting to pick up his things, then remembering he had no things to pick up.

"Hold on, hold on," said Bryan.

"What's the problem?" said Icky.

"If we go to the beach," said Bryan, "everyone might laugh at my eye."

"No one's going to notice your eye!" scoffed Icky.

"No one's going to notice your eye, Bryan!" echoed Stinky.

"Although," added Icky, "they might laugh at your puny white body."

Bryan's face fell. "I'm not ... puny," he mumbled.

Stinky laid a consoling hand on Bryan's shoulder. "You are *quite* puny, Bryan," he said. "And you are definitely very white."

"So are you, under the dirt," said Bryan.

"True," said Stinky, "but people will never see that."

Bryan folded his arms. "I'm not going," he said.

"For Pete's sake!" cried Icky. "If you're so worried about looking like a worm, why don't you just go on the sun-bed for ten minutes?"

"Sun-bed?" repeated Bryan. "What sun-bed?"

"The one in the Uninvited Guest bedroom," replied Icky.

"How did that get there?" asked Bryan.

"It was left there by the last Uninvited Guest," replied Icky.

Bryan wasn't at all convinced about this so-called sun-bed, and even less so when he saw it. "That's too big for a sun-bed!" he declared.

The so-called sun-bed was indeed the size of a double bed, which, according to Icky, was exactly what it was. A double sun-bed.

Bryan lifted the lid. "Where's the lights?" he asked.

"They come on when you flick the little red switch inside," said Icky.

Bryan flicked the switch. Nothing happened.

"It only works when the lid's closed," declared Icky. "You have to get inside, close the lid, then switch it on."

"How do you know all this?" asked Bryan.

"The Uninvited Guest told me," replied Icky. That was actually true, although it had happened in a dream.

"OK," said Bryan. "I'll get in, but only if you do."

"OK," said Icky.

Bryan climbed into the so-called sun-bed, although he insisted on keeping all his clothes on, as this was only a trial run. Icky clambered in alongside him and closed the lid.

"I've just noticed," said Bryan. "There's another switch – a green one."

"Ignore that one," replied Icky.

"It says REVERSE over it," said Bryan.

"So?" said Icky.

"How can a sun-bed have a reverse?" asked Bryan.

"Maybe it makes you white again," suggested Icky.

"Or maybe this isn't a sun-bed at all, and it goes and takes off like a plane or something," said Bryan, who was used to this kind of thing happening in the House of Fun.

"You think too much," said Icky. "Just flick the red switch."

Against his better judgement, Bryan did as requested. There was a soft clunk followed by a quiet high-pitched WEEEEEEEEEEEE. Apart from a gentle vibration, nothing else much happened.

"Where's the light?" asked Bryan.

"It's dark light," replied Icky.

"I feel strange," said Bryan.

"You look strange," replied Icky.

"Is it my imagination," asked Bryan, "or is this box getting bigger?"

Icky considered this. The lid did seem further away. In fact, the longer he looked at it, the further it got. "Maybe you should switch it off now," he suggested.

At this point Bryan made a shocking discovery. "I can't reach the switch!" he cried.

Sure enough, the switch was now way above them, though strangely enough, it looked bigger than when it was close.

"Maybe the box isn't getting bigger," suggested Icky. "Maybe—"

"—we're getting smaller!" cried Bryan.

Time to panic.

"Jump for the switch!" yelled Icky.

"It's miles away!" bawled Bryan.

Icky leapt to his feet, scurried to the side of the box and leapt about like a demented kangaroo, but it was a hopeless cause. The switch was way above him and getting further all the time. It was if they were in a garage, then a warehouse, then a monstrous great aircraft hangar. Soon they couldn't see the roof at all.

"Stinky!" yelled Icky.

"Stinky!" howled Bryan.

There was no response.

"It's no good," said Bryan. "Our voices have gone small as well."

Icky paused for breath. "I think we've stopped shrinking," he said.

"That's something," said Bryan.

"We've just got to turn on the Reverse," said Icky.

"Only Stinky can do that," said Bryan.

"We've got to get to him," said Icky.

Icky scanned round the huge expanse. "The electric lead must come in somewhere," he said. "Maybe we can get out there."

"Over there in the corner," said Bryan.

The two housemates made their way to the far corner of the so-called sun-bed, which was a fair old walk. There they were relieved to find an exit which was, however, really quite scary. The great black wire curved down like the main cable of a suspension bridge, and what lay at the bottom was anybody's guess.

Chapter Eight

Footsore and leg-weary, Bryan and Icky gazed up at the great skaggy sock-toe looming out of the giant shoe like a beached whale.

"Yep," said Icky. "That's Stinky."

"The s-stench," trembled Bryan. "It's f-f-flippin' awful."

"Smells fine to me," said Icky, who, as we all know, had no sense of smell.

"Stinky!" yelled Bryan. "Stinky, can you hear us?"

There was no reply.

"Stinky!" cried Icky. "Dinner's ready!"

Still no reply.

"We're going to have to get to the Ear," said Icky.

"The Ear?" repeated Bryan. "What's *that* going to be like?"

"There's only one way to find out," said Icky.

The two mates began searching for a way into Stinky's shoe. Stinky had often mentioned a hole where water used to get in and all kinds of unpleasant things used to get out, but the two mates had no idea where this hole was. Then, just as they turned the corner of the heel, they caught sight of a great opening like the mouth of a make-believe cave in a monstrous theme park.

But that wasn't all they caught sight of.

"I don't believe it!" cried Icky. "A queue!"

"But ... what are they?" trembled Bryan.

The two mates gawped at the bizarre sight ahead of them. Pale bloated blobs with four pairs of scaly legs … bright red hairy beasts with forked claws around their mouths … creatures like armadillos with the legs of kangaroos … all barging and bustling, chattering and rowing, with one aim in mind – to get inside Stinky's shoe.

"W-what'll we do?" asked Bryan.

"Join the queue, I suppose," replied Icky.

"Are you joking?" said Bryan.

"OK," said Icky. "We'll say there's a medical emergency and push our way to the front."

"I'm not going near those … freaks!" squealed Bryan.

"Just because they're ugly," said Icky, "doesn't mean they're not nice people."

"Whatever they are," replied Bryan, "they are not people."

"You're so stuck-up," said Icky. With that, he sauntered up to the tail of the queue and struck up a conversation with the nearest scaly blob.

Bryan watched from a safe distance. The blob didn't eat Icky, or attack him with its scaly legs, or even sting him with the curly fishing-lines that surrounded its body. In fact, Icky and the blob seemed to be getting on fine.

Bryan edged just close enough to catch the conversation.

"Oh, I'm not keen on the Back End," the blob was saying. "Far too busy at this time of year. The Arm Pit, on the other hand, that's got all the advantages of the Back End without the crowds. *And* there's guaranteed scum, even in winter."

"Have you tried the Belly Button?" asked Icky. "There's plenty of scum there."

"That's true," replied the blob, "but there's

absolutely nothing for the nits to do. You can't enjoy soaking up the scum when the nits are all moaning."

A hairy-backed crab-like thing butted in: "You want to avoid the Belly Button," it said. "The food's terrible."

Note from Blue Soup:

You may be surprised that these microscopic creatures all spoke perfect English (most had a little French as well). In fact, the Spoonheads never bothered to teach such small creatures, but, being parasites, they absorbed the language from their hosts, along with blood, skin scales and so on. Oddly enough, all the parasites spoke in posh accents. The reason for this is unclear.

"Bryan!" yelled Icky. "Come and meet my new friends!"

Bryan reluctantly sidled up to the growing crowd around Icky. "Hi," he mumbled. "I'm Bryan."

The blob tittered. The hairy-backed crab-like thing sniggered. Soon the whole crowd was chortling uncontrollably.

"What's up?" said Bryan huffily.

"I'm sorry," replied the blob, struggling to control tears of laughter. "It's just ... your eye!"

Bryan looked round the circle of grotesque and misshapen life-forms and felt suitably miffed. "Actually," he said. "I had an accident."

The blob laid a hairy segmented claw on Bryan's shoulder. "Looks aren't everything," it said consolingly.

By now the queue had edged up to the entrance, giving Icky his first view of Stinky's foot. It was a great teeming tapestry of life, full of colour and noise, crowds going hither, thither and zither, nits wailing, skin-flake sellers touting their wares, flea taxis fighting for position, and everywhere the scent of new-mown fungus (which, of course, Icky couldn't smell). The blob was warmly embracing a relative, or possibly eating its head, while the hairy-backed crab-like thing was offering a claw to Icky.

"Toodle pip," it said. "We must keep in touch."

"Sure," said Icky. "Er ... how?"

"I'll give you my mobile number," replied the hairy-backed crab-like thing.

Icky took out his own mobile, which (of course) had shrunk at the same rate as he had. "What's the name?" he asked.

"Gerald," replied the hairy-backed crab-like thing.

"Really?" said Icky. "I wasn't expecting you to have such a normal name. What's your surname?"

"Araballawongaflittersnooparroolabarashottabiggamffnplthawooglethingummyandbobbahuckntomnallacriskeenlawnanallaheffalumpasmallaramalamadingdongmolesworthagalooba," replied the hairy-backed crab-like thing.

"I'll just put 'Gerald'," said Icky, tapping in the number Gerald displayed on his own (unusually hairy) mobile.

"Have a good trip," said Gerald. "By the way, where are you going?"

"The Ear," replied Icky.

The whole crowd around Icky fell silent. "The ... Ear?" repeated Gerald.

The circle of creatures backed away. Each one of them had its mouth open, or something which looked like a mouth. "Is there something wrong with the Ear?" asked Icky.

"Don't you know?" asked Gerald.

"Obviously not," replied Icky.

Gerald's voice sank to a whisper: "*Luggug* lives there," he said.

Note from Blue Soup:

It is impossible to write the name "Luggug" accurately, but if you know the noise made by water just before it disappears down the plughole, you will have a fair idea of what it sounds like.

"Who's Luggug?" asked Icky.

No one seemed prepared to answer. Icky's new friends prefered to talk about pleasant things, like fishing around for a vein to suck on, or burrowing into some nice soft skin to lay some eggs.

"Who's Luggug?" repeated Icky.

Icky's new friends carried on with their small talk, slightly louder than before. Gerald took Icky quietly to one side. "Listen, friend," he said.

"If you want to go up to the Ear, that's your business. But don't drag us into it."

"I was hoping for a lift," replied Icky.

"No chance," said Gerald. "Unless ..."

"What?"

"How desperate are you?"

"Very."

Gerald indicated with a hairy claw. "Up there by the toes," he said, "you'll find Lame Jack Chigger. Runs tours where no one else will go. But be warned – Lame Jack's a law to himself. Don't mess with him, or he'll make a horrible mess of you."

"Cheers, Gez," said Icky. "See you later then."

"Goodbye, Icky," replied Gerald.

At this point Bryan finally arrived on the scene. "What's happening?" he asked.

"Good news," said Icky. "We're going on a fun tour."

Chapter Nine

Lame Jack Chigger hobbled up on his one good leg and squinted at the housemates through his one remaining eye. "The Ear?" he rasped. "Sure, I'll take you to the Ear. But it'll cost you."

Bryan searched through his pockets. "I have some rare and interesting stamps," he announced.

"Don't take no stamps," snarled Lame Jack.

"That's a shame," replied Bryan, fighting the urge to correct Lame Jack's grammar. "What *do* you take?"

"Blood," rasped Lame Jack.

Bryan shuddered. Lame Jack really was an ugly character, with his bulbous red body, his one leg hanging off, his three arms chewed to ribbons, and the pale green slime which dripped constantly from his gaping mouthparts.

"Hmm," said Icky. "Blood could be tricky. How much are you after?"

"How much have you got?" snapped Lame Jack.

"Just enough thanks," replied Icky.

"No deal," rasped Lame Jack.

That appeared to be the end of the matter, except Lame Jack had been bored for a while now, and really did feel like some company. "I'll tell you what," he said. "You seem like a funny pair of guys. How do you fancy entertaining me?"

"Sure," said Icky.

"This is the deal," said Lame Jack. "You keep me entertained all the way to the Ear, and I'll do the trip for free."

"Frabjous!" said Icky. "Let's go!"

"Hang on," said Bryan. "What if we *don't* keep you entertained?"

"Well," replied Lame Jack, "I have this little stinger which paralyses you. Then, while you're still awake but totally helpless, I drain all the blood out of you."

"Sounds fair to me," said Icky.

"Eh?" said Bryan.

"We'll entertain him, easy," whispered Icky.

"Climb aboard, boys," said Lame Jack, slapping the side of the saddest, most broken-down flea in the universe.

Icky and Bryan got their feet into the stirrups and swung their legs over the back of the flea, which groaned under their weight. Lame Jack leapt up behind them, which almost brought the flea to its knees.

"Get on, you useless tyke!" yelled Lame Jack, and the flea set off, not in leaps and bounds, but with a dismal foot-dragging shuffle.

It was going to be a long journey.

Note from Blue Soup:
Some of you may be wondering what Stinky was doing all this time. Well, obviously, he was looking for his housemates, which involved a lot of frantic rushing around in circles. Icky and Bryan, however, were completely unaware of this. After all, the Earth spins round the Sun at 67,000 miles an hour, but it doesn't make you fall over, does it? Enough science, back to the story.

Icky had a huge store of jokes dating back to the 1830s, a few of which were hilarious, most of which were so-so, and some of which were downright painful. As the flea-bus crawled drearily up Stinky's leg, Icky began rattling them off with great enthusiasm. Lame Jack didn't actually laugh at any of the punchlines, but he did laugh heartily at all the cruel and violent bits, which encouraged Icky no end. Had he taken his time, he could have easily joked his way to the shoulder, or even the neck, but of course Icky never took his time about anything, even when his life depended on it. By the time the flea-bus reached the belly, he was running out of material fast.

"Do you want to see my tricks?" he suggested. "I can go boss-eyed, or sew up my mouth with invisible thread."

"No tricks," rasped Lame Jack. "More jokes."

Icky strained and strained, and finally dredged a joke from the seabed of his head. He nudged Bryan. "Knock knock," he said.

"Who's there?" asked Bryan.

"Interrupting Cow," said Icky.

"Interrupting Cow wh—" began Bryan.

"MOOOOOOOOOOOOO," said Icky.

There was short pause, which was not filled with laughter. "You never let me finish the question," complained Bryan.

"No, that's the joke, see?" explained Icky. "I'm Interrupting Cow, so I interrupt you, see?"

"I don't care what you are," said Bryan. "It's rude to interrupt."

"Is this part of the joke?" snarled Lame Jack.

Icky thought quickly. "No, we're doing a play now," he said.

"Are we?" said Bryan.

"The kind you make up as you go along," explained Icky.

"This had better be good," rasped Lame Jack.

"So, Bryan," said Icky. "Have you got any nice thistles for me to eat?"

"Thistles?" echoed Bryan. "There's no—"

"Yum! These taste nice!" said Icky.

"You interrupted me again!" complained Bryan.

"It's part of the play!" hissed Icky.

"Oh," said Bryan.

"This is the last time I visit your field," said Icky.

There was a brief pause. "Is that part of the play too?" asked Bryan. "Or are you really saying it?"

"It's part of the play!" hissed Icky. "Honest, you're useless!"

There was another brief pause. "That's part of the play too, is it?" asked Bryan.

"No," replied Icky. "I'm really saying that."

Lame Jack pulled the flea to a sharp halt. "Shut up," he rasped. "You're beginning to bore me."

A tingle of fear tickled the housemates.

"I know!" said Icky. "I can make farting noises with my armpit."

"Get off, the two of you," ordered Lame Jack.

Icky and Bryan slid obediently to the ground,

followed by Lame Jack, who inspected the pair of them like a sergeant-major. "You," he said, pointing at Bryan. "You've let your pal do all the talking so far. *You* entertain me."

Bryan thought for a moment. "What do you get," he began, "when you cross a horse with a donkey?"

"A honkey?" suggested Lame Jack.

"A mule," replied Bryan.

Lame Jack frowned. "Is that a joke?" he asked.

"No," replied Bryan. "It's a fact."

"Facts aren't entertainment!" roared Lame Jack.

"I believe they are," replied Bryan.

"Entertainment," declared Lame Jack, "is you banging your head on a skin tag, or falling down a pore."

"I can be amusing and interesting in many ways," countered Bryan, "without making a fool of myself."

"Now I'm getting really bored," said Lame Jack. With that, he seized Bryan by the shoulders and pinned him down with a claw of steel.

"W-what are you doing?" trembled Bryan.

"Nice knowing you," rasped Lame Jack.

Before Bryan's startled eyes, a long bendy injector arched down from Lame Jack's mouthparts.

"N-n-n-n-n-n-o-o-o!" cried Bryan. With terror-driven strength he broke free of Lame Jack's death-grip, squatted like a frog, and with hands on knees began a wonky-legged loony dance while yodelling at the top of his voice:

"Oh, we're riding along on the crest of a wave
And the sun is in the sky!
All of our eyes on the distant horizon,
Look out for passers-by!"

At this point Bryan ran out of words, but carried on boldly with six verses of animal noises, followed by a wobbly jelly impression, a waddling duck, and a thumb-sucking baby wanting Mummy.

The performance ended with Bryan rocking gently, thumb still in, asking if anyone had seen his malted milks.

Lame Jack, who'd been baffled at first, now viewed Bryan with total fascination. "That's the funniest thing I've ever seen!" he declared. "What else do you do?"

Bryan sprang to his feet and adopted the expression of a village idiot. "Der ... I don't know, boss," he garbled. "I don't know nuttin about nuttin. I'm Hodge the farm hand, I am."

"Then harvest me some blood for my flea," said Lame Jack.

"Sure thing boss," replied Bryan. "Is that full-fat, or semi-skimmed?"

"Clotted, you idiot!" said Lame Jack.

"I got you, boss," replied Bryan, then had a second thought. "Are you really calling me an idiot," he asked, "or is that part of the play?"

Lame Jack snarled. "Forget it," he said.

"I get confused," said Bryan.

"I used to be a fantastic actor," said Lame Jack. He held up his horribly chewed arms. "Till this happened," he added.

"Why did that stop you acting?" asked Icky.

"Don't ask me," said Lame Jack. "Ask the others."

"I can see why you can't be a Romantic Lead," said Bryan. "But what about Character Parts?"

"Shut up about it now," rasped Lame Jack.

Bryan buttoned his lip. Icky, on the other hand, forged right ahead. "What *did* happen to your arms?" he asked.

There was a long silence. "You'd think I'd stay away from the Ear," mumbled Lame Jack. "But I'm drawn back there, again and again and again, like a louse to a hairy forest."

Icky put two and two together. "Did Luggug have your arms?" he asked.

There was an awful, unearthly groan from Lame Jack. "Curse that devil's spawn!" he cried.

"I'll take that as a Yes," said Icky.

Lame Jack's one good eye fixed on the house-mates with grim resolve. "You have entertained me well," he said. "Now I will strike a new deal with you."

"Fire away," said Icky.

"I will take you to the Ear," rasped Lame Jack, "and you will bring me the head of Luggug."

Chapter Ten

Not a word was spoken on the rest of that day's journey. Lame Jack's mind was fixed on the vile creature that had mangled his arms, and the house-mates were simply too nervous to talk.

The flea-bus plodded on, past the Belly Button bypass, over the Great Rash, through the Upper Abdomen oilfield. Finally, in the shadow of the Great Boil, Lame Jack pulled his mount to a halt.

"We camp here for the night," he barked.

Bryan and Icky climbed off to admire the majestic sight before them.

"Who'd have thought there'd be a snow-capped mountain on Stinky?" mused Bryan.

"Actually," said Icky, "I don't think that's snow."

"Relax," said Lame Jack. "It hasn't erupted for years." He scraped up a clawful of dried blood, fed his flea, then settled down for the night, leaving the housemates to scout around for supper. Luckily there was a small lake of dried baked bean not far away.

Note from Blue Soup:

The following scene, like the one in Chapter Six, will appear in the major motion picture to be produced by the Wacky House team. By now you will know what to expect, so prepare yourself with a good sturdy sick-bag.

Moonlight flickered over the Great Boil as Neville Nerd tossed another stick on the campfire. Widget sat nearby, a bowl of beans in his hands, lost in thought.

"Mind if I join you?" asked Neville.

"Be my guest," replied Widget.

Neville sat down, and after a few seconds, took out a photograph. "That's my girl," he said.

Widget studied the photo. "She's very pretty," he replied.

Neville sighed. "We've been thinking about settling down," he said.

"Neville Nerd, settle down?" laughed Widget. "That'll be the day."

"I mean it, Widget," replied Neville. "I've had enough of life on the road. We're going to get ourselves a piece of land, raise a family ... who knows, maybe even make our own jams and pickles."

"I guess that does sound kinda nice," mused Widget.

Neville's face became grave. He removed a gold ring from his finger and handed it to Widget. "Widget," he said. "If I don't make it through this, I want you to give this to Arabella."

"Who's Arabella?" asked Widget.

"My girlfriend!" replied Neville.

Widget pushed the ring away. "This is crazy talk," he said. "Of course you're going to make it."

Neville supped nervously at his drink. "We don't know what's up there in that Ear," he said.

Widget's eyes met Neville's. He could not disguise his own fears. "Let's get some shut-eye," he murmured. "We need all the rest we can get."

Note from Blue Soup:

Relax, everyone. Now we go back to reality.

Next morning was dark, gloomy and tinged with doom. Lame Jack Chigger and the housemates moved warily up the neck, in the shadow of the overhanging hair, which was bestrewn with the strangest flotsam and jetsam imaginable. Far off they heard the excited chatter of nits and the twittering of stray aphids. But their minds were focussed on one thing and one thing alone: Luggug.

At length the three reached the back of the Ear and began the great ascent to the lobe. Lame Jack cursed and cracked his whip at the poor old flea, who staggered and wheezed its way to the summit. Then, finally, they got their first glimpse of the long descent down to the Earhole. That was as far as Lame Jack was willing to go.

"Remember our deal," he said. "You bring me that devil's head. Woe betide you if you fail me."

Icky and Bryan listened well, because if there was one thing they didn't want, it was to be betided by woe. Then they set off, armed with nothing but their wits and a large pirate's cutlass given them by Lame Jack. At first they tried to walk, but soon realised it was easier to slide down Stinky's Ear as if it were a helter-skelter. As they approached the great cavern of the Earhole, however, the mounds of wax made the going tough.

"Maybe if we shouted now," said Icky, "Stinky might hear us."

"Too risky," said Bryan. "What if he doesn't hear us, but Luggug does?"

"That's true," said Icky. "We need the Element of Surprise."

Right now, however, it was the Element of Wax that was the problem. Entering into the cavern, the housemates found it harder and harder to pull their feet from the clammy orange gunk. The further they plodded, the deeper it became, till they were almost up to their knees in it. Then, suddenly, as Bryan struggled to move forward, he lost his balance completely.

"Icky! Help! I'm falling backwards!" he cried, arms windmilling madly.

Icky waded as fast as he could towards his stricken comrade, and with a mighty heave sent him back upright – except the heave he gave was just a bit *too* mighty. For a brief second Bryan's windmill arms circled madly in the opposite direction, then, with an awesome FLUBBB, he toppled face-first into the beastly syrup.

"Nnnnbbllrggh!" he gulped, staggering to his feet like a half-melted candle.

"Ssh!" hissed Icky. "What's that?"

Something else was stirring in the wax. The whole floor seemed to swell and bubble, until a living form began to separate itself from it. First, a giant globe of a head, with blind swollen eyes, then a waxen neck, stretching and shrinking like a giant slug, and finally a body like a twisted rubber tyre, with stunted limbs ending in bloated tree-frog fingers. The grotesque form rocked and rolled in a strange agony, like a mortally wounded worm, before opening a mouth which was a perfectly circular sea of teeth.

"Who is in my chamber?" it groaned, and even its voice was a waxen rumble.

"It's blind!" hissed Icky.

"But I hear perfectly," groaned the waxen beast.

Icky gestured Bryan towards him and whispered almost silently into his ear: "Let's get round the back and jump him."

"*Perfectly*, I said," growled the beast. "Attack me at your peril."

With the Element of Surprise lost, the two housemates were in a critical position. Bryan had often read about positions like this in great legends, and knew exactly what to say: "We have business in the Inner Ear," he proclaimed, "and seek safe passage."

There was a pause. "Step forward," commanded the beast.

Icky stepped up.

"Not you," groaned the beast. "The one who spoke."

Quivering with dread, Bryan waded forward through the wax until he could smell the strangely sweet breath of the beast.

"Let me feel you," growled the beast.

Before Bryan could object, the beast's swollen sticky fingers were dabbing and jabbing all over him. "You're not a louse," it groaned. "You're not

a tick. You're not a chigger. What are you?"

"My mum once said I was a nit," quivered Bryan.

"You're like no nit I've seen," replied the beast.

"But you can't see," said Icky.

"I see with my fingers," croaked the beast.

"That's clever," gabbled Bryan, hoping to get on the beast's good side.

"It is the Way of Nature," replied the Beast. "Once I saw with my eyes, but my touch was blind."

"I'm sorry to hear that," said Bryan.

"Stand back now," groaned the beast. "I want to feel the other one."

Icky was in a difficult situation. The cutlass was in his hand, and the beast was sure to hear if he laid it down. As he stepped forward, he handed it silently to Bryan.

"*What passed between you?*" groaned the beast.

Icky froze.

"*Something passed between you!*" moaned the beast. "*What was it?*"

"It was ... a banana," gabbled Icky.

"A ba-na-na," repeated the beast. "I do not know a ba-na-na."

"It's a long yellow thing," replied Icky. "You eat it."

"There is no smell of food," groaned the beast.

"Are you good at smelling too?" asked Bryan, in his best creepy voice.

"My sense of smell is perfect," replied the beast. "And by the way, you two stink."

"What do you expect?" said Icky. "We're standing on Stinky."

There was a pause.

"The Glommos?" groaned the beast. "You call the Glommos 'Stinky'?"

"Stinky is our friend," explained Icky.

At these words, the beast's whole manner seemed to change. Its head tilted to one side and its voice softened. "That is my view," it murmured.

"H-how do you mean?" asked Bryan.

"All of us take from the Glommos," replied the beast. "But I believe we should give something back."

"That sounds fair," said Icky.

The beast growled. "Of course it is fair!" it groaned. "But it is more than that. If we do not give back to Glommos, Glommos will weaken and die.

And all the parasites will die with him."

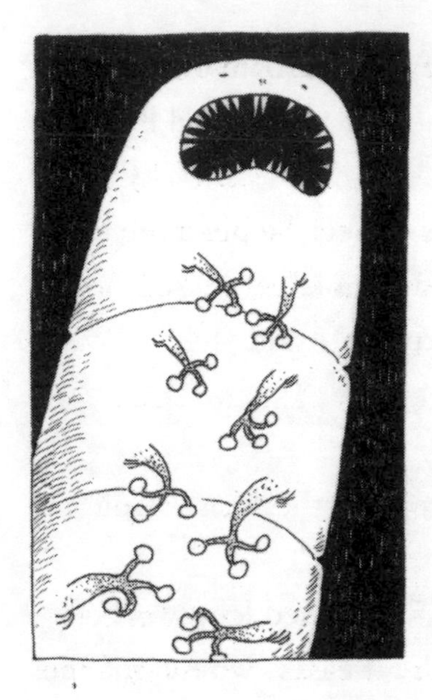

Bryan applauded enthusiastically. "Well said!" he crowed.

Suddenly the beast reared up. "Are you laughing at me?" it boomed.

"No! No!" cried Bryan. "I really mean it!"

The air was tense and dangerous as the beast weighed up Bryan's true meaning. "I came here," it groaned, "to escape the laughter."

"I'm really not laughing," said Bryan, although he was wetting himself in another sense.

"Why did the others laugh at you?" asked Icky.

"Why?" replied the beast. "Because they are stupid! Because they did not want to hear what I had to say! Because they are so busy with their blood-sucking and their egg-laying, they do not want to think about what they are doing to Glommos!"

"Is that why you chewed Lame Jack's arms off?" asked Icky.

"Ha!" scoffed the beast. "That is typical of the lies they tell about me!"

"So you didn't chew them off?" asked Icky.

"I have hurt nobody," replied the beast.

"So … you won't be hurting us?" asked Bryan hopefully.

"Why should I hurt you?" replied the beast.

Bryan began to relax.

"Unless," added the beast, "you intend to hurt me."

Bryan's hand twitched nervously on the cutlass.

"Do not judge by appearances," continued the beast. "I was not always the monster you see before you. I was forced to live here amongst the wax, and in time, I became a creature of wax."

"We know how you feel," replied Icky. "We moved into this nutty house, and now we're nuts."

"You will never know how I feel," groaned the beast, and with that began to tell his whole story, a story so long and complicated that afternoon passed into evening and Icky and Bryan began to feel very tired, but not as tired as the beast itself, whose voice grew slower and slower, till it was like the drawl of a run-down tape.

"I have needed to speak," it finally groaned, "and now I must rest."

So saying, the beast rolled on to its side, laid down its head, and became silent.

Bryan and Icky could not believe their luck.

"Is it really asleep?" whispered Bryan.

"Let's see," whispered Icky.

The housemates crept nervously up to the beast's ear. "Luggug!" hissed Icky. "Luggug, can you hear us?"

There was no movement or reply.

"It's spark out," whispered Icky.

Bryan checked for himself, but there was no doubt about it. The monster was dead to the world. "You'd better have this," said Bryan, offering Icky the cutlass.

"Why me?" said Icky.

"I've got a verruca," replied Bryan.

"Let's just shout for Stinky," suggested Icky.

"And wake Luggug?" replied Bryan. "You must be mad."

"He's not going to hurt us," said Icky.

"So he says," replied Bryan. "Besides, what if Stinky still can't hear us? We've still got to face Lame Jack."

Icky drew a deep breath. "But Luggug's done nothing wrong," he said.

"If you believe him," replied Bryan.

"I do believe him," said Icky.

"Anyway," said Bryan, "if we were normal size, we wouldn't think anything of squashing a bug."

"But we're not normal size," replied Icky.

"We will be soon," said Bryan, "if you just chop Luggug's head off."

Icky folded his arms. "You're the one that's keenest to do it," he said.

"Keen*er*," corrected Bryan.

"There you go then," said Icky. "You do it."

This was going nowhere, time was moving on, and the beast might wake at any minute. Bryan knew there would never be a better chance to complete the mission. "All right," he said finally. "But when we get back, you make sure everyone knows that I was the hero."

With that, Bryan raised the cutlass into the air. The blind beast still did not stir, its great head lying still and peaceful on its waxen bed.

Icky turned away.

Bryan drew a deep breath.

Then

EEEEEAAAAAAA!

"*W-what's that?*" trembled Bryan. The cutlass dropped from his hand. The beast awoke. All three gazed in shock and awe at the monstrous form that suddenly filled the Earhole.

"Luggug!" cried the beast.

"What?" gasped Icky. "*You're* Luggug!"

"What are you talking about?" cried the beast. "*That* is Luggug!"

Without further ado, the beast that was not Luggug began burying itself in the wax, sinking speedily out of harm's way. Meanwhile the real Luggug retreated for a moment, then thrust itself brutally back into the tunnel towards the cowering housemates. It was the shape and size of a submarine, with a great jagged roof overhanging it, under which was a forest of filth and fungus.

"Spare us!" cried Bryan. "Spare us, O great Luggug!"

The brutal monster drew back once more, then lunged again, missing the housemates by a mere fraction. In the gloom of the Ear Canal, it was just possible to see the bizarre ridges over its nose, like swirling furrows in a ploughed field.

"We're done for!" cried Bryan.

Icky, however, remained strangely quiet and calm. "I could be wrong," he declared, "but I think that's Stinky's finger."

Bryan's face became quizzical. "Do you know," he said, "I think you're right."

The more the housemates looked, the more obvious it became.

"Jump on to the end of it!" cried Icky. "It's the safest place to be!"

With that, Icky leapt up at the monstrous digit, followed swiftly by Bryan. There they clung for their lives as the colossus surged on towards the great door of the Eardrum.

Note from Blue Soup:
You may wonder how Bryan and Icky managed to attach themselves to Stinky's finger. If so, you have not been paying full attention to previous chapters.

"He must be able to hear us now!" cried Bryan. "We're miles inside the Ear!"

Icky drew a deep breath and hollered like a lost mountaineer. "Stinky!" he cried. "It's us! It's Icky and Bryan!"

There was a pause, then an awesome voice like a rumble of thunder. "Icky? Bryan? Where are you?"

"We're on the end of your finger!" cried Icky.

Suddenly the darkness disappeared and Icky and Bryan found themselves sweeping through space at fantastic speed, winding up eye-to-eye with an eyeball the size of a cathedral.

"How did you get there?" boomed a thundery and much-amazed voice.

"It's a long story!" cried Icky, but his voice was lost in the great cosmos of Stinky.

"Hang on," said Stinky. "I'll put you back in my ear."

"N-o-o-o-o-o-o!" cried Bryan, as they swept back through space, re-entered the darkness, and plunged again into a sea of wax.

"Stinky!" cried Icky. "You must take us back to the sun-bed, which isn't a sun-bed at all by the way, and put us on the green switch, and close the lid, and stand well clear!"

"You're still using too many 'ands', Icky," muttered Bryan, but his advice was quickly forgotten as the daylight flooded back and the wind whistled past their faces like an express train.

Just as instructed, Stinky was lowering them into the sun-bed-that-wasn't and scraping them gently off on to the green switch. Being on the end of this switch was a bit like being on a high diving board, one which rose towards the sky and stood a giddy height above an empty pool.

As the lid to the sun-bed-that-wasn't began to close, Icky took command. "Jump!" he cried. The two housemates leapt in the air, then thumped back down. The switch quivered but stayed upright.

"Jump harder!" cried Icky. The housemates leapt like demented elephants, there was an almighty CRACK, and the switch shot downwards with such sudden speed that Icky and Bryan were sent tumbling into the abyss below. But just as it seemed they had finally sealed their fate, all the far things suddenly became close things, all the big things suddenly became small things, and the housemates found themselves alive, well and normal-sized, though almost crushed to death by about seven other bodies.

"At last!" groaned a pudgy boy in Bermuda shorts.

"Did they shrink you as well?" asked a swotty girl with pigtails.

"Let's just get out of here, shall we?" said Bryan.

With some difficulty, the whole crowd unpeeled themselves and climbed out of the sun-bed-that-wasn't, before the amazed eyes of the legendary Stinky Finger.

"So," said Icky. "Anyone fancy a holiday?"

Chapter Eleven

Icky put the final touches to his sandcastle while Bryan checked it over for historical accuracy. The beach was littered with sandcastles of different shapes and sizes, tended by dozens of happy young fingers.

"This is the best holiday ever," said Icky, to a chorus of agreement.

"Do you want to play beach cricket again?" asked Bryan.

"My legs are still sore from hopping," replied Icky. "You be the beach cricket this time."

"Maybe Stinky will do it," suggested Bryan.

"Where is Stinky, by the way?" asked Icky.

Bryan stood up and looked around. He really did have a lovely chestnut tan now. What a shame he'd forgotten to take off his sunglasses and looked a bit like a raccoon. "I hope he's not doing you-know-what," he said.

"We'd better find him," said Icky.

Icky and Bryan set off across the beach, over the headland, and through the lily pools to no-man's-land. They found Stinky exactly where they expected to find him, bouncing around on a wall of air with sparks flying everywhere.

"Stinky!" cried Icky. "You know you're not supposed to play with the force field!"

"But I like it!" moaned Stinky.

"You'll blow all the fuses again," warned Icky.

"Besides," added Bryan, "you might electrocute your parasites."

"You can talk!" said Icky. "You were going to chop the wax monster's head off."

"I wouldn't *really* have chopped his head off," said Bryan, with a guilty quiver of the eyes. "And *anyway*, if I had've done, at least it would have got rid of Stinky's itch."

"I've decided I like my itch now," said Stinky.

"That's convenient," replied Icky.

The three housemates began strolling casually back towards the beach, which, as you will have gathered by now, was the latest product of the Super Safari Viewing Lounge.

"I wonder if Lame Jack's still waiting for us," mused Icky.

"We could get a microscope and find out," suggested Bryan.

"Let's not bother," said Icky.

"You really should consider having a wash, Stinky," said Bryan.

"OK," said Stinky.

Bryan stopped in his tracks. "You'll have a wash?" he gasped.

"No," said Stinky. "I'll consider it."

The three housemates strolled on, till the

beach came back in view, with all their new mates playing happily.

"Why don't we just stay on holiday?" suggested Icky.

They thought about this.

"But if we stayed on holiday," said Stinky, "it wouldn't be a holiday any more."

"That's true," replied Icky. "It would be normal life."

There was a long pause.

"OK," said Stinky. "I've considered it."

"What?" said Icky. "Staying on holiday?"

"No," said Stinky. "Having a wash."

Icky and Bryan waited for Stinky's next words, but it was a long wait.

"And your conclusion is?" asked Bryan.

"Oh," said Stinky. "Was there supposed to be a conclusion?"

"Never mind," said Bryan.

"It's the journey that counts," said Icky.

Stinky's brow furrowed. "What does that mean?" he asked.

"I don't know," replied Icky. "It just seemed the right thing to say."

"It's the journey that counts," repeated Stinky. "I like that."

In a pleasant thoughtful glow, the three housemates padded back down to the beach, to soak up the sun, to reflect on their amazing day, and to enjoy the many delights of the Super Safari Viewing Lounge. When it came to getting away from home, there was no place like home, but only when your home was Stinky Finger's House of Fun.

More adventures with Stinky and friends!

STINKY FINGER'S HOUSE OF FUN

Jon Blake

The Spoonheads have arrived in their space-hoovers and sucked up all the grown-ups! So Stinky and Icky will never have to change their underwear again.

In search of an Aim in Life, the two great mates head off to Uncle Nero's House of Fun. But soon they're being besieged by an army of pigs who want to make people pies!

They're going to need more than Icky's lucky feather and Stinky's smelly pants to save their crazy new home ...